Lee Aucoin, *Creative Director*
Jamey Acosta, *Senior Editor*
Heidi Fiedler, *Editor*
Produced and designed by
Denise Ryan & Associates
Illustration © Shelley Dietrichs
Rachelle Cracchiolo, *Publisher*

Teacher Created Materials
5301 Oceanus Drive
Huntington Beach, CA 92649-1030
http://www.tcmpub.com
Paperback: ISBN: 978-1-4333-5570-7
Library Binding: ISBN: 978-1-4807-1715-2
© 2014 Teacher Created Materials
Printed in China
YiCai.032019.CA201901471

Way Back When

Written by Helen Bethune

Illustrated by Shelley Dieterichs

Ethan burst into the kitchen, where his grandfather was sitting with his laptop.

"Hey, Grandpa, can I interview you for my school project? I have to find out what sort of things you did when you were my age."

3

Grandpa laughed. "Ethan, you would not believe how different things were way back when. Why, when I was your age, I—"

Ethan interrupted. "I'm sorry, Grandpa, but I've already figured out a list of questions. Can we stick to those?" Ethan had his pencil and notebook ready.

5

"Sure, Ethan. Let's see what you've got!" said Grandpa.

"First, what games did you play at my age?" asked Ethan.

"Let's see. We played baseball and basketball. I was in Little League," replied Grandpa.

"I'm in Little League, too! What else?"

"We played with Frisbees, marbles, and jacks.
I had the most cat's eyes in my grade," said Grandpa.
"I had 32 of them."

"No one at school plays marbles. What are cat's eyes?
Oh, forget it. You had Frisbees? Wow! I love playing
Frisbee with Scout. What are jacks?"

9

Grandpa said, "I'll draw one for you. You need a set of them. Then, you need a hard surface and a little bouncy ball…"

"Can we look it up online, Grandpa? Then, I could get a better idea."

"Probably. Everything's on the Internet. That's something very different from my day."

"You kids never need to go to the library to look up information, or even read a book. You just look it up online."

Ethan looked surprised. "I read books! That was my next question. What were your favorite books when you were my age?" Grandpa ruffled Ethan's hair. "I know you read books."

Grandpa continued, "Well, I really liked Dr. Seuss's *Green Eggs and Ham* and *The Cat in the Hat*—just like you. And I liked *The Saggy, Baggy Elephant*. That's the one we read together just the other week. And I really liked comics. Every week, I spent a dime on them," said Grandpa.

15

"That's cheap! Did you read ninja comics?" asked Ethan. "They're great. But they cost four dollars each. What computer games did you play?"

Grandpa sighed. "No, ninja comics weren't around then. And neither were computer games. In fact, computers hadn't been invented."

"But you had electricity, didn't you?" Ethan asked.

"What do they teach you in school? Yes, we had electricity! Thomas Edison invented the light bulb in 1878."

Ethan grabbed his calculator. "That's more than 135 years ago!"

"Yes," said Grandpa, "But we didn't use calculators. We did have television, but it was in black and white."

"TV was in black and white! Wow!" Ethan rolled
his eyes. "I guess you didn't spend much time watching
it then.   It must have been really boring."

"You're right, Ethan. We didn't spend much time watching television. There weren't lots of shows for kids then. My friends and I spent our time riding our bikes around the neighborhood, going down to the stream, and catching tadpoles.

"Your parents let you do that? Ride around on your own?" Ethan asked.

Grandpa replied, "There weren't so many cars in those days, Ethan. It wasn't as dangerous."

"What sort of car did your family have?" Ethan asked.

"We had a Ford Fairlane. It had a huge hood, a V-8 motor, and my dad got 10 miles to the gallon out of it. That's an awful lot of gas, but it was cheap then, and people didn't realize the effect those cars were having on the environment."

"Look, I'll show you a picture of one," said Grandpa. Ethan gazed at the car.

"Wow! Did your mom drive you to school in it? That would have been awesome."

"No, we caught the bus to school, just like you do. I think those buses have been around forever."

24

Ethan looked at his list of questions.

"Grandpa, I think I've got enough information now to do my project. I only had to ask you five questions, but I've got more answers than that. You've been a big help. Thank you!"

26

As Ethan started to leave the kitchen, he turned to his grandfather and said, "You know, Grandpa, even though lots of things were different way back then, lots of things are still the same. That's kind of nice."

Grandpa smiled.